Sea Food

or

Who eats who in the ocean

by

Charles Messing

To my wife,
Lissa Messing,
for her love, friendship, and support

Introduction

The "Walrus and the Carpenter"
was written long ago
and told of how the two of them
lured oysters in a row
from quiet, weedy oyster beds
and ate them, don't you know.

Though this is not the way things work
beneath the salt sea air,
it took a lot of oysters just
to satisfy that pair,
and that's the rule when all kinds of
sea creatures take their share.

We start with great big numbers at
the bottom of the heap,
with algae and seaweeds and plants
that never live too deep,
because their pigments need the bright
sun's energy to reap.

Then up the sea life pyramid
our hungry way we wend,
and every step along we chop
one zero off the end.
But, go ahead and read this little
book that I have penned.

The Open Ocean
Part 1

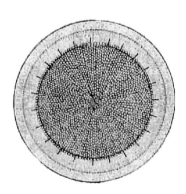

10,000

TEN THOUSAND tiny diatoms
are glistening golden cells
that soak the brilliant sunshine up
inside their glassy shells.

Pinhead
(0.04 in or 1.0 mm across)

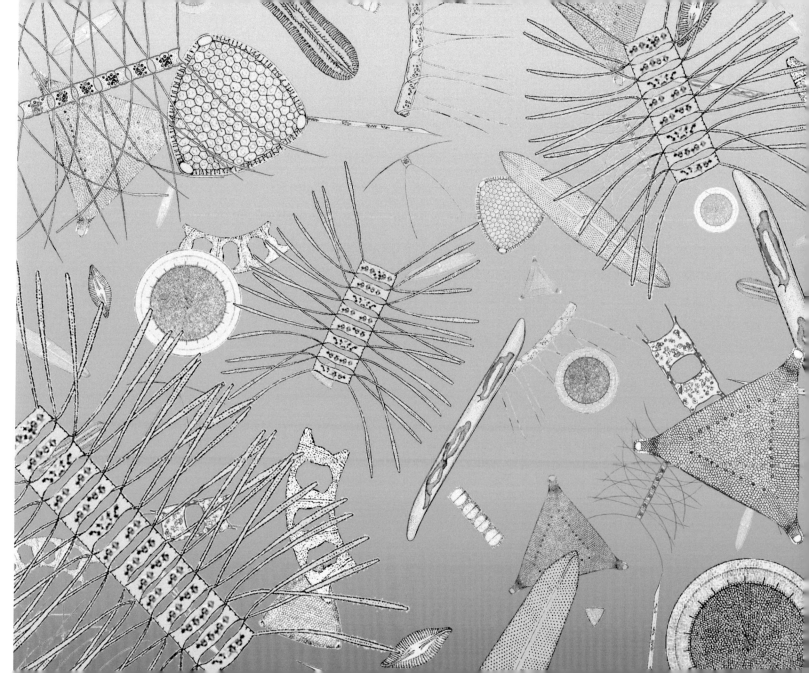

1,000

ONE THOUSAND copepods dart by
like insects in the foam.
They grab those cells with fuzzy feet,
each one a fine-toothed comb.

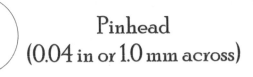

Pinhead
(0.04 in or 1.0 mm across)

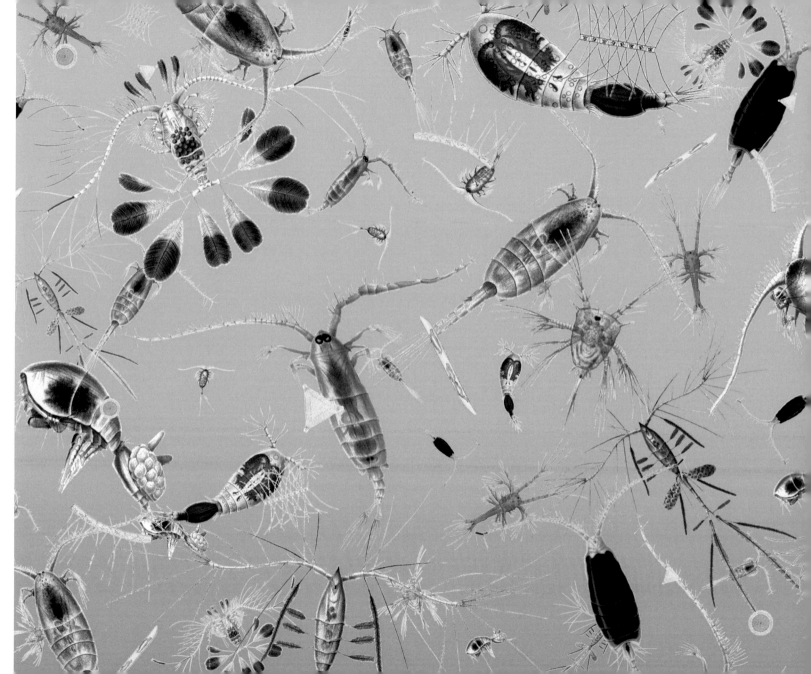

100

ONE HUNDRED silver sardines
have copepods for lunch.
They swim quite close together in
a school, a gang, a bunch.

Number 2 pencil
(7.5 in or 19 cm long)

10

TEN squids' appendages*
have rows of suckers neatly placed.
They're jet-propelled so fast that
not one sardine goes to waste.

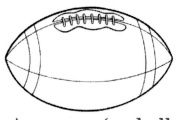

American football
(11 in or 28 cm long)

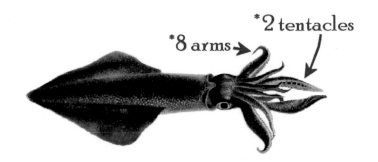

*2 tentacles

*8 arms →

1

ONE sperm whale needs a lot to eat
and so is never sorry
to dive a mile beneath the waves
to dine on calamari*.

*When squid appears on your dinner table
it often carries this Italian label.

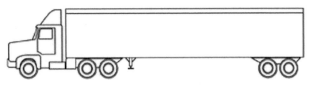

Standard tractor~trailer
(57 ft or 17.5 m)

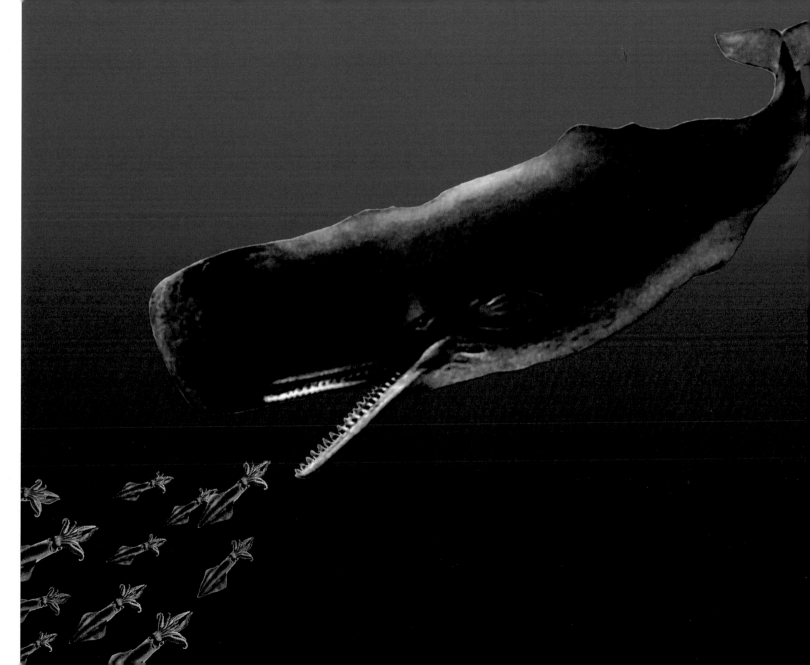

A Rocky Seafloor

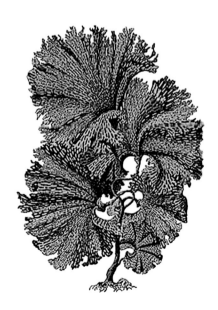

20,000

4d nail
(1.5 inches)

Soft waving seaweeds grow in groves
upon a rocky bed,
where TWENTY THOUSAND show their colors:
green and brown and red.*

*Some seaweeds grow longer than a basketball court,
while others are tiny; in other words, short.

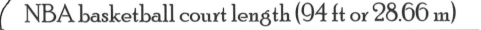

NBA basketball court length (94 ft or 28.66 m)

2,000

TWO THOUSAND fat round sea urchins
have spines that they wave and turn.
They graze on seaweeds with sharp jaws
called Aristotle's Lantern.

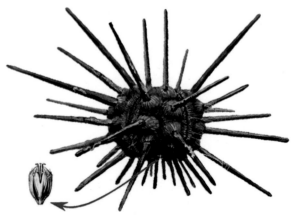

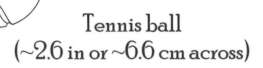

Tennis ball
(~2.6 in or ~6.6 cm across)

200

Each of TWO HUNDRED crusty lobsters
have two kinds of nippers.
The stout ones crunch the urchins' shells.
The thin ones act as rippers.

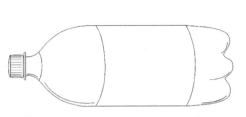

2-liter plastic soda bottle
(12.5 in or 31.75 cm long)

20

Shhh. TWENTY eight-armed octopuses
each have a private den.
They pounce out, grab a lobster supper,
then retreat again.

FIFA World Cup soccer ball
(~8.6 in or ~22 cm across)

2

Through the sea TWO silent sharks
glide through the dim dawn's light,
and eight soft arms are no match for
sharp teeth and appetite.

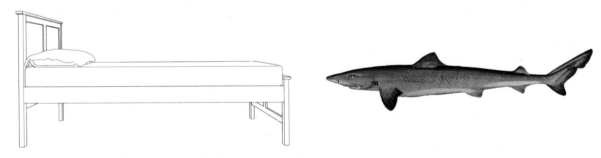

King size bed (80 in or 2.44 m long)

Cold Antarctic Ocean

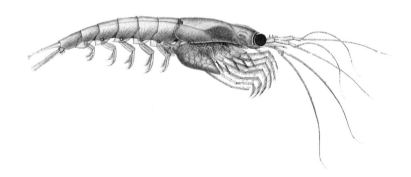

30,000

Now THIRTY THOUSAND diatoms
create a shimmering sight.
Their spines and oils* keep them from sinking
down below the light.

*Their spines spread their weight out to either side
like a backfloat with arms spread open and wide.
And, a droplet of oil inside of each one
is lighter than water, so they stay near the sun.

Newspaper period
(0.01 in or 0.3 mm across)

3,000

In cold Antarctic waters live
the shrimp we call the krill.
THREE THOUSAND feed on diatoms
and always eat their fill.

U.S. 1-cent coin
(0.75 in or 19.05 mm across)

300

When penguins waddle on the ice,
you'd never call them trim.
But when THREE HUNDRED dive for krill,
it's certain they can swim.

Standard U.S. mailbox
(~19 in or ~48 cm long)

30

Among the mammals that have fins
and swim with graceful motion,
these THIRTY leopard seals behave
like lions in the ocean.

Basketball
net height
(10 ft or 3.05 m)

3

The sea's great predators include
THREE killer whales, and when you
have such big teeth, then even leopard seals
are on your menu.

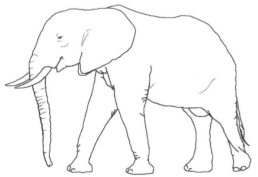

Male African elephant
(~20 ft or ~6.1 m head to tail)

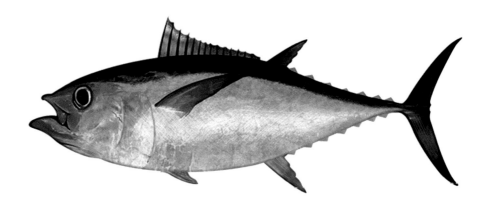

The Open Ocean
Part 2

40,000

Though FORTY THOUSAND whirling cells
need sunlight, we just can't
consider dinoflagellates
as animal or plant. *

*Creatures of one cell, scientists noticed,
belong in their own group, which they call the protists.

Thickness of a U.S. 1$ bill
(0.004 in or 0.11 mm)

4,000

Sea butterflies are snails that swim
beneath the clear blue ocean.
FOUR THOUSAND flap and feed on cells
with one wing-footed motion.

U.S. 10-cent coin (dime)
(0.705 in or 17.91 mm)

400

Up from the depths at night come
hatchetfish that glow and glimmer.
FOUR HUNDRED eat sea butterflies
and other little swimmers.

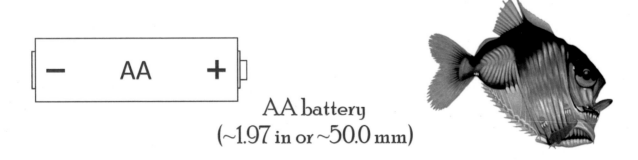

AA battery
(~1.97 in or ~50.0 mm)

40

Then FORTY streamlined big-eye tuna
swim so fast, it's blurring.
They'll feed on hatchetfish, or squid,
or lanternfish or herring.

Average adult
American male
(5 ft 10 in or 1.77 m tall)

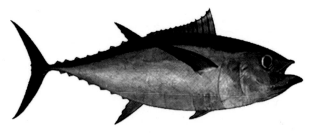

4

FOUR friends at lunch know tuna is a fish that tastes good and which can be served as a salad, or a casserole or sandwich.

But, simple chains are not quite true – we must make a correction.
A food web better demonstrates the intricate connections.
To demonstrate just who eats who is very complicated.
Each creature feeds on far more things than I have illustrated.
Some copepods are predators that feed upon their cousins.
And, the kinds of prey some fish consume are counted by the dozens.

More names and more creatures ⟶

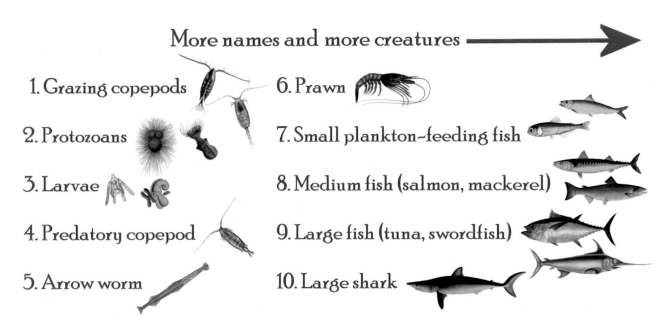

1. Grazing copepods

2. Protozoans

3. Larvae

4. Predatory copepod

5. Arrow worm

6. Prawn

7. Small plankton~feeding fish

8. Medium fish (salmon, mackerel)

9. Large fish (tuna, swordfish)

10. Large shark

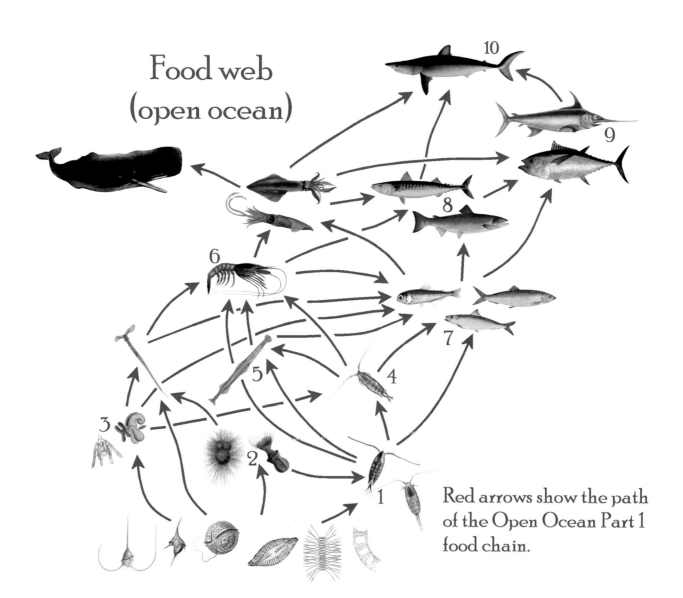

Food web
(open ocean)

Red arrows show the path
of the Open Ocean Part 1
food chain.

Glossary

Algae (AL-jee) – Organisms that carry out photosynthesis but are not true plants. (True plants are the mosses, ferns, grasses, herbs, shrubs, flowers, and trees.) They can be red, brown, gold, blue-green, or green. Most algae are protists, but green algae are sometimes classified as simple plants, and blue-green algae are actually bacteria. Algae range from one-celled, microscopic diatoms and dinoflagellates to huge brown algae taller than many trees. Algae is plural; alga (AL-guh) is singular.

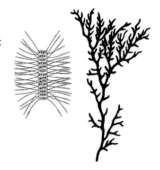

Appendage – A part of an organism that sticks out from the body and has its own structure and purpose. Legs and arms are appendages. A squid has 10 appendages—8 arms and 2 tentacles. An octopus has 8 appendages, all arms (no tentacles).

Aristotle's Lantern – The complex chewing jaws of a sea urchin.

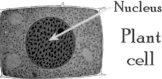

Cell – The basic unit of life. Living things made of one cell, such as diatoms and protozoans, do all life requires, such as eating, growing, and swimming. In living things with many cells, whether a fish, seaweed, lobster, or you, different cells do different things – blood cells carry oxygen, stomach cells digest food, and skin cells protect the body.

Nucleus

Plant cell

Copepods (CO-peh-pods) – Small crustaceans that are major links in ocean food webs. Copepod means "oar-footed", because most use their appendages to row through the water.

Crustaceans (Cruh-STAY-shuns) — Animals with segmented bodies, segmented appendages, and a tough protective outer covering. They are related to insects and spiders, but they have two pairs of feelers. Copepods, lobsters, shrimps, prawns, and crabs are crustaceans.

Diatoms (DIE-ah-toms) — One-celled, golden algae that produce a glassy shell. Diatom means "cut in two", because their shell is in two pieces.

Dinoflagellates (Die-no-FLAY-jeh-lates) — One-celled algae with two whip-like swimming appendages called flagella. Most are photosynthetic. Dinoflagellate means "whirling little whip", because they swim in spirals.

← Flagella

Larva — An immature stage of an animal that does not look like the adult. Many ocean animals hatch from an egg as a larva and spend time drifting as plankton before becoming a juvenile that is strong enough to swim (fish), or settle to the sea floor (sea urchin, lobster). Some animals remain so small as adults that they stay in the plankton (sea butterfly, arrow worm). Larva is singular; larvae (LAR-vee) is plural.

Sea urchin larva

Snail larva

Microscopic — Too small to see with your eyes. (You need a microscope.)

Organism — An individual living thing – animal, plant, fungus, protist, or bacterium.

Photosynthesis (Foe-toe-SIN-theh-sis) — A process inside algae and plant cells that uses water, carbon dioxide, and the energy of sunlight to build sugars that store the energy. It also produces most of the oxygen in the air we breathe. Digesting the sugar releases the energy to carry out life's activities: growing, moving, making babies, and building other substances such as fats and proteins.

Pigment – A colored substance. Pigments in algae and plant cells collect sunlight for photosynthesis.

Plankton – The smaller, drifting organisms in the ocean. Plankton in this book includes diatoms, dinoflagellates, copepods, krill, sea butterflies, protozoans, arrow worms, some prawns, and larvae (of larger organisms, including fishes, lobsters, and sea urchins).

Prawn – A common name for certain kinds of shrimps.

Protists (PRO-teests) – Organisms (except the animals, fungi and true plants) constructed of complex cells with a nucleus that contains the DNA. Most protists are microscopic (such as diatoms, dinoflagellates, and protozoans), but seaweeds are also protists. Bacteria and their close relatives have no nucleus and form separate groups.

Protozoa – Chiefly one-celled protists that were once considered simple animals, mostly because they could swim around.

Seaweeds – Plant-like algae large enough to see with your eyes.